HILLTOP ELEMENTARY SCHOOL

EARTH MOTHER

Ellen Jackson

Illustrations by Leo & Diane Dillon

Walker & Company ✺ New York

Earth Mother awoke with the dawn. She fanned sacred smoke in each of the four directions.

Then she walked across the land singing a morning song.

Earth Mother gave the beetles shiny jackets. She hung green acorns on the oaks.

Bending low, she placed a piece of summer in a flower's seed.

She turned her gaze to the sage-covered deserts and blew across the mesas.

A hawk cupped the warm air with its wings.

Man greeted Earth Mother as she walked beside the river.
He held a net in his hands to catch frogs for his breakfast.

"You are kind to me, Earth Mother," said Man. "You have
sent Frog to fill my belly and I am grateful."

Man slapped at his face.

"But why have you sent this wretched Mosquito to torment me—to sting me at night and drive me from my bed?" he asked.

"Mosquito is bad, bad, bad. Frog, on the other hand, is sweet, tasty, and oh-so-wonderfully delicious. If there were more frogs and no mosquitoes—none at all—this world would be perfect."

Man went back to the business of hunting for frogs.

Earth Mother walked on.

Earth Mother walked across the African savannah
wearing a robe fringed with falling rain.

She filled the water holes and sharpened the
thornbushes. Her hand guided a sunbird to a blossom
sweet with nectar.

She climbed a peak and flung a spear of lightning into the sky.

The mountains felt the sting and fury of her storm.

In the north, Earth Mother powdered the trees with snow. Tiny crystals gleamed in the air like diamond dust.

In the late afternoon, Earth Mother heard Frog calling. Frog sat on a rock near a lake. With a flick of his tongue, he caught a small insect and swallowed it whole.

"Thank you, Earth Mother," said Frog. "Mosquito and her
sisters fill my belly and give me life.

"But why have you sent Man to catch and eat me? Man is bad, bad, bad. Sweet, delicious Mosquito, on the other hand, makes me happy. If there were more mosquitoes and no men, this world would be perfect."

Earth Mother smiled and walked on.

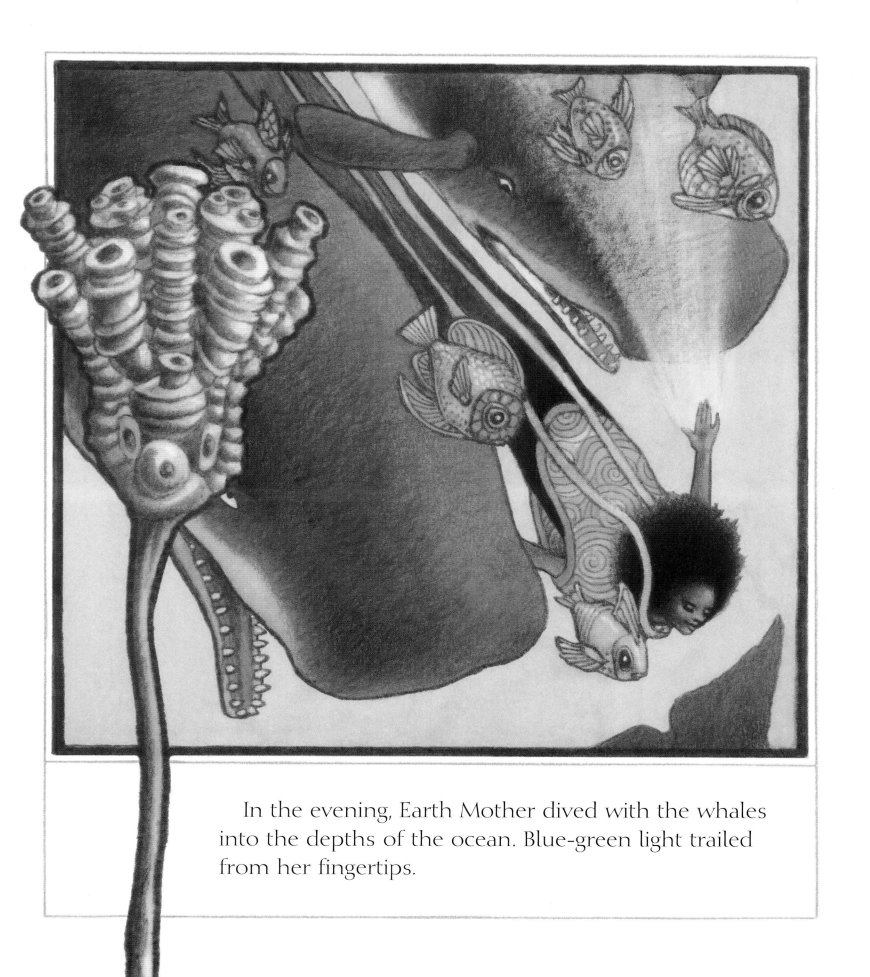

In the evening, Earth Mother dived with the whales into the depths of the ocean. Blue-green light trailed from her fingertips.

A silver moon rose on the horizon.

Earth Mother cradled an otter in a tangle of seaweed,
rocking him on the waves.

It was nighttime. As Earth Mother walked through a meadow, she heard a tiny voice.

"Earth Mother, it is I, Mosquito," said the owner of the voice. "Frog will surely feast on me tomorrow or the next day. He has already caught most of my sisters.

"But I am grateful for Man who lives by the river. He is tender and delicious when I bite him in his bed. What's needed is more men and none of those useless frogs. Then this world would be perfect."

Earth Mother sighed. Once more she walked on.

Earth Mother climbed the hill to her cloud tepee.
She spangled a tree with fireflies.

She spread spiderweb lace on the grass.

Earth Mother said good night to the beetles, to the
hawks, to the people, to the sunbirds, to the frogs, to the
whales, to the otters, to the mosquitoes, to the fireflies,
to her children everywhere.

Then she went to sleep. . . . And the world, in its own way, was perfect.

To my wonderful editor,
Tim Travaglini —E. J.

To Tim, Lee, and Greg —L. & D. D.

First published in the United States of America in 2005 by
Walker Publishing Company, Inc.
Distributed to the trade by Holtzbrinck Publishers

For information about permission to reproduce selections from
this book, write to Permissions, Walker & Company,
104 Fifth Avenue, New York, New York 10011.

Library of Congress Cataloging-in-Publication Data

Jackson, Ellen B., 1943–
Earth Mother / Ellen Jackson ; illustrations by Leo & Diane Dillon.
    p. cm.
    Summary: Portrays a day in the life of Earth Mother, who, as she tends plants and animals
around the world, meets three of her creations with advice on how to make the world more
perfect.
    ISBN 0-8027-8992-7 (HC) — ISBN 0-8027-8993-5 (RE)
    [1.Nature—Fiction. 2. Earth—Fiction. 3. Food chains (Ecology)—Fiction. 4. Day—Fiction.]
I. Dillon, Leo, ill. II. Dillon, Diane, ill. III. Title

PZ7.J13247Ea 2005
[E]—dc22

                                                                        2004061201

ISBN-13 978-0-8027-8992-1 (hardcover)
ISBN-13 978-0-8027-8993-8 (reinforced)

The artists used watercolor and colored pencils on watercolor paper to create the
illustrations for this book.

Book design by Nicole Gastonguay

Visit Walker & Company's Web site at www.walkeryoungreaders.com

Printed in Hong Kong

10 9 8 7 6 5 4 3 2 1